Witch You Were Here

Kate Saunders worked as an actress until she was twenty-five and then became a writer. She has written five novels and edited a collection of short stories. As a journalist she has worked for the *Sunday Times*, the *Daily Telegraph*, the *Independent* and the *Sunday Express*, and is currently writing a weekly column in the *Express*. She can be heard regularly on BBC Radio 4, presenting *Woman's Hour* and appearing on *Start the Week* and *Front Row*. She lives in London and has a six-year-old son.

The *Belfry Witches* titles are Kate's first books for children. A major BBC TV series is based on them.

Titles in The Belfry Witches series

All Belfry Witches titles can be ordered at
your local bookshop or are available by post
from Book Service by Post (tel: 01624 675137).

The Belfry Witches

Witch You Were Here

Kate Saunders
Illustrated by Tony Ross

MACMILLAN
CHILDREN'S BOOKS

For Leonora and William

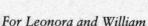

First published 2000 by Macmillan Children's Books
a division of Macmillan Publishers Limited
25 Eccleston Place, London SW1W 9NF
Basingstoke and Oxford
www.macmillan.com

Associated companies throughout the world

ISBN 0 330 37286 6

Copyright © Yellowbeetle Ltd. 2000
Illustrations copyright © Tony Ross 2000

The right of Kate Saunders to be identified as the
author of this work has been asserted by her in accordance
with the Copyright, Designs and Patents Act 1988.

3 5 7 9 8 6 4 2

A CIP catalogue record for this book is available from
the British Library.

Typeset by SX Composing DTP, Rayleigh, Essex
Printed and bound in Great Britain by Mackays of Chatham plc, Kent

Contents

1

Away From It All

In the vicarage garden, in a quiet village called Tranters End, two witches were rainbathing. This is what witches do instead of sunbathing. Like frogs and snakes and other leathery-skinned creatures, they don't like too much sun.

One of the witches – Old Noshie – smiled as she felt the cool raindrops pattering on her head. "Cor, this is lovely!" she said. "We've had such nasty hot weather lately." She popped a passing spider into her mouth.

Skirty Marm lay back comfortably in her deck chair. "I've never understood what the humans see in that sun," she declared. "Nasty, vulgar, flaming thing – thank goodness for rain! Ah, this makes me think of old times!"

Both witches sighed, remembering the beautiful damp chilliness of their old home. Old Noshie and Skirty Marm had grown up on

Witch Island, which is a bleak and rocky place. The weather is usually wet, and the sun is always hidden behind a thick grey duvet of cloud. Nowadays, they lived happily in the church belfry at Tranters End, and dearly loved the humans of the village – but they still missed the Witch Island weather.

Mrs Abercrombie, the wicked Queen of Witch Island, had banished Old Noshie and Skirty Marm for one hundred years, because they had committed a dreadful crime. They had sung a rude song about Mrs Abercrombie at the Hallowe'en Ball (see *The Bumper Book of Famous Rude Songs*, Belch & Squelch, 9w. shillings). The two homeless witches had found shelter in Tranters End, and the local people were now quite used to occasional bursts of magic.

"Where is everyone?" wondered Skirty Marm. "It's a shame to be stuck indoors on a gorgeous day like this!"

"Mr B. and Alice have taken Thomas into town," said Old Noshie, picking spider-legs out of her teeth. "Mr Snelling's in the study – and goodness knows where Mendax has got to. I haven't seen him for days."

Mr Babbercorn was the young curate of St Tranters Church. He lived at the vicarage, with his wife Alice and their baby son, Thomas. The Babbercorns were the witches' best human friends. They had been bridesmaids at the wedding of Mr B. and Alice, and they were little Thomas's godmothers. Old Noshie and Skirty Marm were also extremely fond of the vicar, Mr Snelling – a very kind, very plump and rather greedy man.

Mendax was the vicar's adopted cat. He had once been a cat-slave on Witch Island, and he could talk (which was upsetting for strangers). In fact, Mendax talked all the time. He did the shopping, cooking and cleaning, and bossed the vicar from morning till night.

Skirty Marm snorted scornfully – she never could forget that Mendax had once been a spy, working for Mrs Abercrombie.

"That cat is up to something!" she declared. "He's been acting very strangely ever since he went back to Witch Island for that weekend break."

"He keeps sneaking off to the shed," Old Noshie agreed. "He's put black paper over the window so nobody can peek inside."

"He needn't be so SNOOTY!" sniffed Skirty Marm. "Whatever he's up to, I wish he'd let us join in! It's been so boring here since the Power Hat left."

Old Noshie shuddered. "I'm glad it's gone. If this is boring, it suits me fine."

The Power Hat had caused a lot of trouble for the witches in the past, and put them in terrible danger. It was a witch's hat, two metres tall, with an everlasting candle burning at its point. No living witch knew all its secrets, but its magic was immense. The witch who wore the Power Hat was the strongest witch in all the world and, until Old Noshie and Skirty Marm returned to Witch Island after their banishment and stole the Hat, it had belonged to Mrs Abercrombie.

Without it, she was nothing more than an extremely clever but ordinary old witch. For the first time, the witches of the Island had a proper election and threw out their evil queen.

Since then, Mrs Abercrombie had spent all her huge fortune trying to snatch the Power Hat back, but Old Noshie and Skirty Marm had always managed to keep it out of her evil hands. You will not be surprised to hear that Mrs Abercrombie now hated the two witches. She swore that she would kill them the minute the Hat was back on her head and her gigantic bottom was back on the throne.

Then, last Hallowe'en, the Power Hat had burst into flames and VANISHED.

Nobody knew what had happened to Mrs Abercrombie. She had not been seen since, by witch or human – but she often appeared in the nightmares of Old Noshie and Skirty Marm. She was hugely fat, and her terrible wickedness made her ugly face even more hideous. Her chin was covered by a straggly grey beard (usually full of half-digested insects), her teeth were made of metal and her eyes were little and curranty, and incredibly mean.

It made Old Noshie shiver just to think of her. "When Mrs A. was chasing that dratted Power Hat," she said, "I never had a minute of peace. I was always scared she'd suddenly pounce on me!"

Old Noshie was a plump, easy-going witch, with a bald head, which she usually covered with a blue wig, and a skin of startling bright green (she glowed in the dark, and the vicar often used her to find things in the cellar). She was not particularly clever, and not at all brave.

But Skirty Marm was always getting mixed up in dangerous adventures – and Old Noshie had never done anything without Skirty Marm. She had followed her faithfully, since the pair were little witches at school.

Skirty Marm was a long, skinny witch, with fizzing red eyes and a clump of purple hair. At school, she had won every prize going – including the Spitting Shield, the Golden Broom and (for thirty-six years in a row) the Spellbinder's Medal. It was hard for a talented witch like Skirty to give up magic, but Mr Babbercorn did not approve, and she had promised to cast no more spells without his permission.

Mostly, she kept her promise pretty well. Instead of brewing potions, Skirty Marm spent her time working for Brownie badges and learning songs at the Old Folks' Drop-In Club. She and Old Noshie were allowed to belong to both the Brownies and the Old Folks' Club because of their strange mixture of ages. Although they were both over one hundred and fifty years old, which is ancient for a human, they were only young Red-Stocking witches.

If you want to know the age of a witch, take

a good look at the colour of her stockings. Here is a simple guide:

1. YELLOW-STOCKINGS – baby witches, under 100 years old, still at school.
2. RED-STOCKINGS – witches over the age of 100 years.
3. GREEN-STOCKINGS – witches over the age of 200 years.
4. PURPLE-STOCKINGS – witches over the age of 300 years.

Generally speaking, if you come across a witch in purple stockings, you should take extra care. Some of the senior witches on Witch Island were many hundreds of years old (Mrs Abercrombie was nearly a thousand), and they came from the days of the old fairy tales, when witches really were very wicked. Like many elderly people, they did not take kindly to changes. Many of the Purple-Stockings, and some of the Greens, hated the newly elected Red-Stocking government of Witch Island. They missed the good old days, when they had been allowed to keep cat-slaves and bully the younger generations.

Skirty Marm did not miss those grim times,

7

but she was finding her non-magical life with the humans far too quiet.

"Nosh, do you know what I'd like now?" she blurted out suddenly. "An ADVENTURE!"

"I wouldn't," said Old Noshie. "Adventures are scary."

Before Skirty Marm could argue, a woman's voice called, "Witches! Biscuits!"

Alice, a smiling young woman with curly brown hair, stood at the back door of the vicarage. Mrs Abercrombie had once turned Alice into a snail, and the witches had saved her.

She had grown very fond of them and often bought them treats.

The two witches loved human biscuits. They leapt up at once and rushed into the kitchen, making wet tracks all over the floor.

"Sorry," said Old Noshie. "We've been RAINBATHING."

"Never mind," said Alice. "Have a Jammy Dodger – I know they're your favourites."

"Hello witches!" shouted Thomas, in his high chair. He was nearly a year old, and he could say two words in English ("cat" and "Daddy"). But he spoke another language – a series of burbles and squawks known as Babyspeak, which both the witches knew.

"Quick, Noshie!" Thomas cried, in Babyspeak. "Get me a biscuit while she's not looking! She won't let me have another, because I keep throwing them on the floor!"

"Don't give Thomas a biscuit," Alice said, without turning round. "He'll only throw it on the floor."

Alice did not know Babyspeak, and did not need to.

Mr Babbercorn was making tea for himself and Alice, two cups of muddy pond water for the witches, and a beaker of juice for Thomas. He was a pale, weedy young man. Today, his thin face was anxious. Both he and his wife seemed rather nervous.

When they were all sitting round the table, he cleared his throat.

"Witches, there's something we want to tell you," he announced. "Alice and I – well, we've decided to take Thomas away for a summer holiday. It'll be our first holiday as a real family. We're off to Gusty Bay, where we went for our honeymoon." He faltered, and his pale face turned red. "The thing is, witches, we – er – we won't be taking anyone with us."

There was a long silence. Both Mr Babbercorn and Alice looked uncomfortable.

Old Noshie said, "Good idea – we don't need anyone else."

Skirty Marm's red eyes were fizzing dangerously. "You silly old PLOP," she growled. "He means he DOESN'T WANT US!"

"*What?*" Old Noshie could not believe her green ears.

"Please don't be offended!" begged Alice. "Two weeks on our own – it's not much to ask!"

"I've been looking jolly pale lately," said Old

Noshie in a very offended voice. "Two weeks by the sea would put the cabbages back in my cheeks."

"Don't expect kindness from these SELFISH humans!" stormed Skirty Marm. "All they care about is having a good time without us. We'll be stuck here, in horrible blazing sunshine, and they'll be living it up on a rainy beach!"

Old Noshie's lips began to wobble. "It's not fair, and you're being very MEAN. We wouldn't be any trouble!"

"I'm afraid not," Mr Babbercorn said, gently but firmly. "The Sea Breeze Guest House doesn't take witches."

Skirty Marm scowled. "You should have booked one that said 'witches welcome'."

"It doesn't mean we don't love you," Alice said. "All we want is a little time on our own. Away from it all."

Skirty Marm leapt up, tossing her purple hair proudly. "Come, Noshie. Let us not dirty our rags in this SMELLY place. We know when we're NOT WANTED."

Skirty Marm stomped out of the house, followed by Old Noshie, who was crying noisily. Her wails could be heard all the way up the one

11

hundred and eighty-six belfry steps.

"Are we being selfish?" Alice asked her husband fearfully. "I feel awful!"

Mr Babbercorn squeezed her hand. "Don't worry. They'll soon get over it."

The witches were scandalized and outraged. How could Mr Babbercorn and Alice dream of taking a holiday without them? The sheer selfishness of it amazed them. They were sure everyone in the village would agree and feel very sorry for them – but nobody seemed to think the Babbercorns were being at all unreasonable.

"It does everyone good to get away sometimes," said Mrs Tucker at the Post Office, who was also Brown Owl. "I'm off to Spain next week."

Even Mr Snelling, who had not been invited to Gusty Bay either, refused to take the witches' side.

"A change is as good as a rest," he said. "I'm going on holiday myself, you know."

"But you never go away!" cried Skirty Marm.

Mr Snelling smiled. "I'm going to stay in a castle in France and have very posh cookery lessons."

"Ha!" snapped Skirty Marm rudely. "Mendax will never allow it!"

"As a matter of fact," said the vicar, "it was his idea."

"What? Eh?" Skirty Marm was instantly suspicious. Mendax hated letting the vicar out of his sight, in case he took up with another cat.

"That little cat is so considerate!" Mr Snelling went on happily. "He says it'll do me good to get away from it all, at the same time as the others. He says he'll hold the fort here – he's even arranged for Father Baggins from St Martin's to take the services!" He giggled suddenly. "It'll

13

certainly do me good to get away from Mendax's nagging. Oh, I can't wait – two whole weeks of making fancy pastry, with nobody mewing at me to trim my nose-hairs!"

"Well, don't expect us to hang around here, with nobody but that sneaky little bag of fur!" snapped Skirty Marm. "Noshie and me are having a holiday too. So there!"

Old Noshie gaped – this was the first she had heard of it. But she had the sense not to annoy Skirty Marm by asking questions. She didn't say a word until they were safely back in their belfry.

"How can we go on holiday, Skirt? We haven't got any human money, and holidays cost ever such a lot!"

"Pooh, we don't need *money*!" Skirty Marm said grandly. "We're witches, aren't we?"

"Yes," Old Noshie said, starting to look worried, "but we promised Mr B. we wouldn't do any magic without asking him!"

"Pish and posh!" snarled Skirty Marm. "Why should we keep any promises to that mean curate?"

"He doesn't deserve it," Old Noshie agreed, with a sniff. "But where are we going for our holiday?"

"Gusty Bay, of course!" said Skirty Marm. "That Mr Babbercorn might think he's getting away from it all, but he's not getting away from US!"

2

What Mendax Was Up To

It was a wonderful idea, and Old Noshie and Skirty Marm were very pleased with themselves. Every time Mr Babbercorn or Alice mentioned Gusty Bay, the two witches burst into giggles and pinched each other with secret glee. Deep down, they knew that following the humans on their holiday was not a very kind thing to do, but they were both too angry about being left out to care.

"Mr B. doesn't OWN Gusty Bay!" Skirty Marm declared. "He can't stop us having our holiday there too!"

"No," Old Noshie said, a little doubtfully. "But, Skirty, we don't know anything about human holidays. What sort of luggage will we need?"

Skirty Marm hated admitting she did not know something. "Oh – I expect it'll be just like

Slime Regis."

"Really?" Old Noshie brightened. Slime Regis was the only holiday resort on Witch Island. It was a grim huddle of black cliffs, lashed by rain and buffeted by freezing gales. Skirty Marm had once won a holiday for two there in a burping contest, and they had both loved it. Old Noshie decided that if Gusty Bay was anything like Slime Regis, things were looking up. "What a pity we couldn't bring our swimming-sacks when we were banished."

"Humans take buckets and spades on their holidays," Skirty Marm said knowledgeably.

Old Noshie was puzzled. "Why?"

"I-I don't know," Skirty Marm admitted, with a frown. "We'd better ask Alice. But we'll have to make sure she doesn't find out where we're going. Leave most of the talking to me."

"Righto," said Old Noshie. "I know I'm rubbish at keeping secrets."

Alice was glad the witches had stopped being cross with her – but she was rather puzzled by their behaviour. For one thing, they kept bursting into giggles for no reason that she could see. And they began bombarding her with all kinds of odd questions about the seaside. Alice

17

still felt bad about leaving the witches behind, and she answered them patiently.

"The buckets and spades are for building sandcastles on the beach," she explained.

"A strange custom," remarked Skirty Marm.

"I wish you'd tell us where you're going," Alice said. "It's obviously somewhere beside the sea."

She could not understand why this made the two witches giggle again.

"Yes, it is!" shouted Old Noshie.

Skirty Marm gave her friend a quick biff, to remind her not to tell.

"I'm afraid we can't say where we're going, Alice," she said firmly. "You'd only get JEALOUS."

Mr Babbercorn would have suspected something by now, but Alice was not a suspicious woman.

"Well, I only know about Gusty Bay," she said innocently, "but most seaside places have the same things. I'd be happy to give you advice."

"We'd like to know," Old Noshie said, "what humans wear in the sea."

"Gracious," said Alice, "haven't you ever

seen a swimming costume? Here." She bent
down to pull something out of the washing
machine. "This is the swimming costume I was
wearing when I first met Cuthbert."

Old Noshie and Skirty Marm were staring,
with gaping mouths and eyes, at the tiny piece of
striped material Alice was holding.

"Where's the rest of it?" asked Old Noshie.

"This is all of it," Alice said.

"What – THAT?" shrieked Skirty Marm. The
two witches burst into howls of laughter. They
laughed so much that Alice became a little
embarrassed.

"You can't wear that teeny thing!" gasped Old Noshie. "Everybody will see the shape of your – *ha ha ha* – the shape of your – *hee hee hee* – your BOTTOM!"

The word "bottom" made the witches laugh until they had to lie down on the kitchen table.

When they had recovered, Alice asked curiously, "What do witches wear when they go swimming?"

"A SWIMMING-SACK, of course!" cried Skirty Marm, wiping her eyes. "It's a huge piece of material, with holes for your face and hands and feet."

"You leave your pointed hat in the changing-cave," added Old Noshie. "And your stockings."

"But NOT your bloomers," Skirty Marm said. "Or someone's sure to NICK them."

Alice struggled not to laugh, knowing this would annoy the witches. "Humans find it difficult to swim if they're weighed down by too much material," she said. "And we don't think it's rude to show the SHAPE of your bottom – just your ACTUAL bottom."

This time, realizing she was serious, the witches did not laugh.

Old Noshie's green face was shocked. "Well, don't expect me to go in the sea in one of those teeny stripy things!"

"Certainly NOT," Skirty Marm said firmly. "Humans have no DIGNITY."

Alice could not help laughing now. She tried to turn it into a cough. "Is there anything else I can tell you?"

"What's the food like?" asked greedy Old Noshie.

"Lovely," said Alice. "That's why you take extra spending-money to the seaside – to buy candy-floss and crab sandwiches and ice creams and chips and sticks of rock—"

"Wow!" murmured Old Noshie, licking her green lips.

Skirty Marm was less interested in eating. "What sort of things do you DO at the seaside?"

"Well," Alice said thoughtfully, "when the weather's nice, you sit on the beach, and play in the sea. And when it isn't very nice, you go to the boating-pool, or the amusement arcade on the pier. That's the other reason you need spending-money. For instance, just a short game of Crazy Golf costs fifty pence."

"That sounds good!" Skirty Marm was fascinated. "What is Crazy Golf?"

"It's a bit like ordinary golf," Alice said, "because you have to knock balls into little holes. But in Crazy Golf, the holes are very funny and surprising."

Old Noshie blurted out, "Is the rainbathing good at Gusty Bay?"

Skirty Marm hissed, "Shut up!" and pinched Old Noshie's nose.

"The rainbathing's very good there, I should think," Alice said. She did not seem to have noticed the pinch. "Sometimes it rains so hard that there's nowhere to go except the slide-show at the Town Hall."

"Cor," whispered Old Noshie, "doesn't it sound BRILL?"

"Not half!" said Skirty Marm. And then she remembered what Alice had said about spending-money. Her grey face became gloomy. "But doesn't it sound EXPENSIVE? Excuse us, Alice – we have to look in our piggy bank."

The witches' piggy bank was not a pig, but a little china cottage. This was where they kept their human money. Mr Babbercorn gave them fifty pence a week each. They earned a bit more by doing odd jobs around the village, such as flying up on their broomsticks to clear people's gutters.

Back in the belfry, Old Noshie and Skirty Marm opened the cottage and emptied their savings out on the dusty floor. Skirty Marm counted the coins. When she had finished, she looked gloomier than ever.

"Three pounds and seventy-two pence. That's not going to get us very far. Noshie, we have to find ourselves some more money."

Old Noshie was worried. "But where? Mr B. and the vicar need all their money for their own holidays. We don't know anyone else we can ask – except Mendax."

Skirty Marm's red eyes flashed. "Mendax! Of course!"

It was well-known to the witches that Mendax had a nice bundle of human money hidden away. Mr Snelling had given it to him. Where his cat was concerned, the vicar's head was as soft as his heart.

"Huh! We won't get anything out of Mendax!" Old Noshie said crossly. "You know how mean he is."

Skirty Marm was grinning and red sparks were fizzing in her eyes. Her great mind had begun to plot and plan.

"Oh yes!" she cackled. "But I also know Mendax is up to no good. If we can just find out what it is – we've GOT him!"

Mendax certainly had been behaving very strangely over the past few weeks. The little cat had started disappearing for hours on end. He would come home very late, often covered in odd substances – mud, oil, seaweed, even beetroot soup once – and he never offered a word of explanation. Most unusually for this neat and elegant animal, he had started to be careless about the housework. He forgot the shopping. He mixed up the whites and the coloureds in the washing, and he kept burning dinners.

Mr Snelling and the Babbercorns were too busy preparing for their holidays to take much notice, but the witches were watching Mendax very closely. One evening, they saw him limp into the vicarage kitchen with his back-left paw in a bandage. They were shocked to hear him telling the vicar he had been in a fight with the cat from the Post Office.

"What a WHOPPER!" Skirty Marm said to Old Noshie later. "The Post Office cat is ill with a bad ear – he hasn't even been out for days. This means Mendax is back to his old ways!"

In Latin, "Mendax" means "liar", and it was a very suitable name for this particular cat. He loved to tell stories as tall as skyscrapers.

Now that the witches knew Mendax was hiding something, they watched him like a pair of hawks. Every day, they took it in turns to crouch beside the belfry window, watching the garden shed through a plastic telescope Old Noshie had got for Christmas. But they saw nothing interesting. Mendax stayed at home, resting his hurt paw. He sat on the lawn reading a book, which was very boring to spy on. The witches began to worry that they would never catch him out.

"And then we'll never have enough human money for our secret trip to Gusty Bay!" Skirty Marm said impatiently on the day before the Babbercorns and Mr Snelling went on holiday. "But he must do something soon – that cat is the reason everyone's going away! He made them think of it! He wants them out of the way! Mr B. and the vicar don't realize it, but they're playing right into his crafty little paws!"

Today it was Old Noshie's turn to watch through the telescope.

"Look out – here he comes!" she shouted suddenly.

At last, far below, they saw the little black cat creeping out of the back door of the vicarage, looking extremely shifty and furtive. He was walking on his hind legs, and carrying a plastic bag in his front paws. After a nervous glance around, he darted across the lawn and shut himself in the shed.

"Action stations!" cried Skirty Marm.

The two witches jumped on their broomsticks and zoomed down to the garden. Old Noshie started giggling again.

Skirty Marm nudged her sternly. "Shut up! And stand back while I break this lock."

Mendax had put a stout padlock on the shed door, and he kept the key fastened to his collar. This kept the humans away, but it was no protection against witches. Skirty Marm muttered a simple lock-busting spell, and the padlock flew open.

"AHA!" roared the witches. "CAUGHT YOU!"

They leapt into the shed – then stopped short, and gaped around in amazement.

There was no sign of Mendax. The shed was crammed with deck chairs, garden tools, crusty tins of paint, and the rowing machine the vicar had once bought to make himself slimmer. All this was pushed against the walls. A large space had been cleared in the middle of the floor.

Old Noshie and Skirty Marm rubbed their eyes in disbelief.

"Where did he go?" gasped Old Noshie.

They had seen Mendax creeping in, but now the only clue that he had ever been here was his plastic carrier bag, lying on a pile of flowerpots.

Skirty Marm snatched it, to look inside. "Sandwiches," she said in disgust. "Fish-paste sandwiches! What's going on?"

As if in answer to that question, there was a sudden, blinding flash of white light.

"AARRGH!" shrieked the witches.

The empty space on the floor was now filled with a crazy machine, which looked like a cross between a sledge, a car engine and a dentist's chair. Mendax was perched at the front of this contraption. On his small head he wore a metal helmet covered with springs. He was very startled – and very annoyed – to see the witches.

"Drat," he mewed sourly. "What are you two doing here? Can't a cat have any privacy?"

But the witches were not listening. They had recognized the strange machine at once, though they only knew it from school books and pictures in the Witch Island newspaper. It was so astonishing that they stared at it in silence, for nearly ten minutes.

"Well, well, well!" Skirty Marm said at last. A wicked grin broke out on her grey face. "So *this* is why you keep disappearing! *This* is why

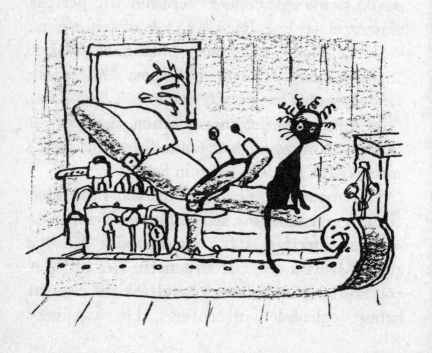

you're so full of secrets! You've got your paws on a TIME MACHINE!"

Old Noshie prodded the Time Machine with her finger. Mendax immediately whipped a little cloth out of his collar and wiped it. "Don't make smears!"

"Sorry," said Old Noshie. "But I've never seen one of these in real life. Where did you get it?"

Mendax was still fiddling with his cloth. He did not seem to have heard.

"OI!" shouted Skirty Marm. "My friend asked you a question! Where did you get this thing?"

"Oh, I picked it up when I had that weekend in Witch Island," Mendax said casually. "It's the new economy model. It comes in a flat-pack, with simple instructions for fitting together."

Skirty Marm laughed unkindly. "Cor, there's an AWFUL smell of LIES in here!"

Like many terrible liars, Mendax was always furious when anyone accused him of lying.

"It's perfectly TRUE!" he snapped. "Look at the box if you don't believe me!"

"You NICKED it," said Skirty Marm, grinning gleefully.

"How *dare* you?" spat Mendax.

"Oh, come off it," Skirty said scornfully. "You know the laws about Time Machines on Witch Island. You need to be a Purple-Stocking, with a special licence signed by the Chancellor. You'd never be allowed to buy one in a million years – so you STOLE one!"

Mendax's bright green eyes flickered from one witch to another. When he spoke again, his voice was very small and sulky.

"All right. I stole it. But I was desperate. I BEG you not to give me away to the Witch Police!"

"We'll have to see about that," Skirty Marm said gleefully. For once, she had Mendax exactly where she wanted him. Stealing a Time Machine was a serious offence on Witch Island. If the Witch Police found out what he had done, no human help could save Mendax from being arrested and sent to prison for ages.

"Where have you been in it?" Old Noshie asked curiously.

"Oh – here and there," said Mendax.

Skirty Marm let out a loud, mocking cackle. "Nosh, I've guessed! I know why he wanted it! Hee hee hee! He's been at the BATTLE OF

FUNGUS GULCH!"

Fungus Gulch was a famous battle in Witch history. It had happened many years before Mendax was born – but this had never stopped him telling stories about how he had been there. At last he had found a way of turning his boastful fantasies into truth.

He scowled. "I suppose you might as well know the whole story. Yes, you're right – Fungus Gulch is the reason I've been away so much."

Old Noshie chortled. "Now you'll have to find something new to lie about!"

Mendax ignored this. "I'm working on something very important. I have to keep going back to the same place in the Battle – because I want to be in the history books. I want to be a FAMOUS HISTORICAL CHARACTER."

"So what are you going to do at Fungus Gulch to get yourself mentioned in the history books?" Skirty Marm asked jeeringly. "A tap-dance?"

"I'll admit," Mendax said, in his most dignified mew, "I've set my sights rather high. I want to lead the Charge of the Pointed Brooms."

This made both witches howl with laughter. The Charge of the Pointed Brooms was one of the most famous incidents in Witch history – rather like the Charge of the Light Brigade in our world. The idea of a small black cat leading the attack was hilarious.

"It's going to take me some time," Mendax said stiffly. "I have to go back again and again, changing the history bit by bit – I'm still trying to get near the front."

"And you wanted the humans out of the way," said Skirty Marm, "because you knew Mr B. and the vicar would be HOPPING MAD if they discovered you tinkering about with such serious magic!"

Mendax's black fur bristled. "Yes, I'm afraid Mr Snelling has some rather old-fashioned notions about magic. I sent him on holiday to stop him asking awkward questions. Now, if you'll excuse me, I must return to the Charge. I only popped back because I forgot my sandwiches."

"Not so fast!" said Skirty Marm. "What's to stop me and Noshie calling the Witch Police and telling the vicar?"

"Oh, I SEE," Mendax mewed icily. "And what do you want for keeping quiet?"

"We'll take the sandwiches, for a start!" said

Old Noshie, with her mouth full of fish-paste.

"And we need to borrow your SAVINGS!" said Skirty Marm craftily.

First, Mendax looked furious. Then he tried to look casual. "My savings? Yes, I do have one or two little coins in my meagre hoard – perhaps twenty pence—"

"Even I know that's a LIE," Old Noshie interrupted cheerfully. "You're the richest cat in the whole village, because you made Mr Snelling PAY you for writing his sermons!"

"You've got a sock stuffed with money!" said Skirty Marm. "You keep it hidden in your cat-duvet!"

"Oh, you've LOOKED, have you?" Mendax snarled.

Skirty Marm put her face close to his. "You have to lend us your money, so we can buy nice things on our holiday."

"We'll pay you back," added Old Noshie. "One day."

Mendax flicked out his claws angrily. "You can go to prison for blackmail, you know!"

"Good, we can all be in prison together," said Skirty Marm.

There was a long, long silence. Then Mendax

sighed, and smoothed his whiskers. "Oh, all right. You can borrow my money. You know where it is."

"Hurrah!" yelled Skirty Marm. "Thanks, Mendax! Have a nice time at Fungus Gulch!" She danced out of the garden shed, beaming like a lighthouse.

Old Noshie had to trot to keep up. She was not beaming, and her breathless voice was worried. "Skirt, if Mr B. finds out we did this, he'll be ever so cross! Crosser than he's EVER been!"

This had already occurred to Skirty Marm, but she was doing her best not to think about it.

"I don't care!" she shouted. "So what if we've blackmailed Mendax? It's all Mr B.'s FAULT for trying to sneak off to Gusty Bay without us!"

"So it is," agreed Old Noshie. "I don't feel at all guilty now. If we do something bad, it's only because he hurt our feelings."

3

The Seaside

There was terrible confusion at the vicarage next morning, with the Babbercorns and Mr Snelling trying to leave for their holidays at the same time. Mr Babbercorn and Alice had borrowed the vicar's car to drive down to Gusty Bay. Mr Babbercorn was loading it with nappies, buckets and spades and picnic baskets, until it seemed about to burst.

Mr Snelling was taking a taxi to the station, where he would catch his train to the airport. He was very flustered and nervous – he had not been away for years, and his ancient luggage was so mouldy that Mendax had made him buy a new suitcase.

Old Noshie and Skirty Marm jumped and laughed and turned somersaults, and got in everybody's way.

"I thought you said you were having a holiday

too," said Mr Babbercorn. "Don't you have any packing to do?"

"We've done it!" said Old Noshie happily.

The young curate had been very busy for the past few weeks, and he had not had time to investigate the witches' holiday plans properly. Now, he looked at them very seriously over the top of his glasses.

"Noshie and Skirty," he said, "I'll tell you the truth – I'm worried about this holiday of yours. It was very kind of Mendax to lend you the money for it, but I'm not sure you can pretend not to be witches for a whole two weeks!"

Alice laughed. "You worry too much, Cuthbert – it'll do the witches good to go off on their own for a change!"

"I'm trusting you both to remember all your promises," Mr Babbercorn said. "No magic, no tricks, no eating mice, no throwing squirrels at each other—"

"No SQUIRREL-CHUCKING?" Old Noshie was disappointed. "That's not fair!"

"It's the kind of thing that scares humans," said Mr Babbercorn, "quite apart from what it does to the squirrels. And it's very unkind to scare people on their holidays. Remember, witches – I'm trusting you to behave!"

Alice strapped Thomas into his car-seat. Then she kissed each witch. "Oh dear, I hate leaving you! Do have a lovely time, wherever you're going! And here's our address, in case you need us – the Sea Breeze Guest House, Railway Bridge Road, Gusty Bay."

"We'll send you a postcard," said Skirty Marm. She spoke cockily because her lip was wobbling. Saying goodbye to the Babbercorns felt awful. Old Noshie let out a sob and blew her nose on her sleeve. Both witches waved and waved as the car drove away down the lane. When it had gone, they stared forlornly at the place where it had been.

"I know we'll be in the same town," said Old Noshie, "but it won't be any good if we can't talk to them!"

The village taxi arrived at the gate for Mr Snelling.

Mendax gave him a lick and turned away to wipe his eyes with the end of his tail. "Have a marvellous time, dear vicar," he murmured. "And don't forget to put your reading glasses back in the right pocket!"

"I'll miss you, Mendax," the vicar said

tearfully. "If you or the witches need me, I'm at the Chateau Gateau, Normandy, France."

He drove off in his taxi, blowing his nose, and the witches and Mendax were left alone in a vicarage garden that suddenly seemed very quiet and sad.

Mendax was the first to recover. "At last!" he said briskly. "I thought we'd never get rid of them. Now I'll be able to work on that battle as long as I like – Time Machine or no Time Machine, I lose my thread when I have to rush back for dinner."

He picked up his bag of sandwiches. "If I don't come back, please look in the history books, to see how I died. It's bound to be SPECTACULAR."

The past and future hero of Fungus Gulch made his way towards the shed.

Old Noshie and Skirty Marm waited at the vicarage until it was dark – they were travelling by broomstick and did not want any human to see them. When the moon had risen in the clear sky, and all the fields were cloaked in blackness, they mounted their brooms in one of the open belfry windows.

It was some time since they had made a long journey by broom. Skirty Marm checked the radio-switches, which would enable them to talk to each other during the flight. Old Noshie checked the supply of Jammy Dodgers.

"Right!" said Skirty Marm. "Brooms – we're heading east, to the town of Gusty Bay!"

With screams of triumph they soared out into the night.

Although the witches did not like hot weather, they found that a warm summer night was perfect for flying. The gentle breezes stroked their rags and cooled their leathery skin. They enjoyed looking down at the sleeping farms and villages below.

After two hours in the air, they landed in a wood to eat their biscuits.

"It's nice to be flying again," said Old Noshie. "Broomsticks are a lot cheaper than trains."

"And it's nice to be free witches," Skirty Marm said thoughtfully. "Not having to worry about being GOOD all the time. Not having to ask Mr B. every time we want to cast a tiny spell!"

"If we're having a holiday from being good," said Old Noshie, "we can play tricks and have

laughs and hurl squirrels as much as we like –
Mr B. and Alice won't even know!"

This was a very exciting idea, and it put both
witches into a frisky mood. Skirty Marm started
the holiday-from-goodness by making her
dribble bright blue and spitting on cars. Old
Noshie terrified some humans in a pub by
suddenly flashing her green face at an upstairs
window. Skirty Marm magicked away a
policeman's clothes and left him shouting
furiously in his underwear. This made them
shriek with laughter.

"Cor, this is as good as Hallowe'en!" cried
Old Noshie.

They decided to halt the naughtiness when
they got close to Gusty Bay. As Skirty Marm
pointed out, "We don't want to attract too much
attention or Mr B. will notice something."

They flew over the ridge of a steep hill, and
both cried, "OOH!"

Ahead of them lay the black rooftops of Gusty
Bay, and beyond them –

"The SEA!" whispered Old Noshie.

For several minutes they hovered on their
brooms in silence. They had never before seen
how smooth and silver a moonlit sea can be.

This was far more beautiful than Slime Regis.

"The water doesn't shout here," said Skirty Marm. "It just sings and sighs!"

The small town of Gusty Bay was very dark and quiet, but the witches saw enough of it to be enchanted. There were coloured fairy-lights along the seafront and on the pier. Large seagulls pecked on the smooth sand. There was a delicious smell of old shellfish.

"We'll take a proper look tomorrow," said Skirty Marm, "when it's light."

Old Noshie yawned noisily. "Where shall we sleep, Skirty?"

"Under the pier looks cosy," said Skirty Marm.

They landed their brooms on the beach. The sand under the creaky wooden pier was damp and covered with clumps of smelly wet seaweed. Old Noshie sat down on it and popped a piece into her mouth.

"Yum – this is lovely!"

Skirty Marm settled herself comfortably against a pillar of wet wood, covered in greenish slime. "Save some for breakfast. Tomorrow's going to be a very busy day!"

*

43

The witches woke suddenly next morning, when a large wave broke right over their feet.

"Drat!" complained Skirty Marm, sitting up on the sand. "My stockings are soaked!"

Old Noshie had been dreaming about Noah's Ark. She was very relieved to find that the whole world was not flooded.

"We'd better put on our human clothes," she said, "before someone sees us!"

Both witches looked around with great interest. The day was grey and rather blustery, with a hint of rain. Above the beach, the shops on the promenade were starting to open – a lady in a pink overall was hanging rubber rings and coloured buckets outside the door of her café. There was a smell of salty dampness.

"Gorgeous weather!" Skirty Marm said happily. She opened the Tesco carrier bag that held her luggage and took out the strange collection of clothes she wore when she needed to disguise herself as a human old lady. Old Noshie covered her green face with white make-up and put on a brown wig instead of her usual blue one. Skirty Marm hid her purple hair under a woolly hat like a tea-cosy, and her fizzing red eyes behind a pair of sunglasses. In a few minutes, the two witches were transformed into two rather bonkers-looking old humans. All signs of witchiness – brooms, musty rags and pointed hats – were safely hidden under a huge clump of seaweed.

"Let's have something special to EAT!" cried Old Noshie. The smells from the café were making her stomach rumble.

"Good idea," said Skirty Marm. She picked up the smart human handbag, which one of her friends from the Old Folks' Drop-In Club had kindly given her, and checked the bundle of Mendax's human money. Both witches were in high holiday spirits. It was still early, and not many humans were about. They went into the café on the promenade and had an enormous breakfast of fried eggs, chips, tomato ketchup, chocolate cake and ice cream, all on the same plate. The lady in the shop was surprised to meet two old ladies with such huge appetites. She was even more surprised when these old ladies bought two rubber rings (one blue, one red with spots) and two fancy plastic spades.

"You won't get much digging done today," she said. "It looks like rain."

"Oh, I DO hope so!" cried Old Noshie. She

thought her spade was so beautiful, she tied it round her neck with a piece of string.

Large spots of rain were falling by the time the witches came out of the shop. Strangely, the humans did not seem to like this weather, and the beach was deserted.

"What shall we do next, Skirt?" asked Old Noshie.

Skirty Marm thought hard. "We could go and spy on Mr B. and Alice," she suggested.

"Great!" cried Old Noshie. "*Heeheehee* – wouldn't they be AMAZED if they knew?"

There was a map of Gusty Bay on the promenade. Skirty Marm, who was good at reading maps, looked for Railway Bridge Road. Old Noshie, who was useless with maps, bought two Mars Bars from a nearby sweetshop, to keep them going. Very happy and excited to be on their first human holiday, the witches set off through the town.

Railway Bridge Road, as you might have guessed, had a railway bridge at one end, and the station at the other.

"Goodness, how POSH!" said Skirty Marm.

The Sea Breeze Guest House was a narrow grey house, with a small front garden and a notice on the door that said "Vacancies".

Old Noshie grabbed Skirty's arm. "Look! I can see them!"

Through the hedge in the front garden, it was possible to see into the dining room. Mr Babbercorn, Alice and Thomas were sitting at a table in the window. Mr Babbercorn was eating a bowl of cornflakes, and Alice was sharing her toast with Thomas. The witches ducked behind the hedge so they would not be seen – this was important, since Mr Babbercorn kept looking out of the window at the grey sky.

"Let's follow them," said Skirty Marm. "They've been here before, so they must know all the nice things to do!"

The witches ate their Mars Bars while they waited for the Babbercorns to finish their breakfast. Presently, the front door of the guest house opened. Shaking with giggles, the witches kept out of sight, behind the dustbins of the house next door. Alice was pushing Thomas in his buggy. The whole family was wearing bright shorts and T-shirts and big raincoats. The unfamiliar sight of the curate without his dog-collar made the witches almost hysterical. Old Noshie had to stuff her wig into her mouth to keep quiet.

"Perhaps it'll clear up later," they heard Mr Babbercorn say. "In the meantime, there's always the slide-show at the Town Hall."

"Oh, well," Alice said cheerfully, "it's better than getting wet."

"Pooh," grumbled Old Noshie. "I wanted them to go to the beach, or play a nice game of Nutty Golf!"

"CRAZY Golf, you old fool!" snapped Skirty Marm. "Do you want the whole world to guess that we're witches?"

Taking great care not to be spotted, they followed the Babbercorns to a large brown building in the middle of the town.

Skirty Marm read the notice outside – *Gusty Bay Town Hall – Slide-Show and Lecture, Today at 10am – Treasures of Italy*.

They were very pleased to find that it did not cost anything to get in.

"What a bargain!" said Skirty Marm happily.

The witches had never seen a slide-show. The big hall inside the building was very dark and nearly empty. A man was projecting brightly coloured pictures on to a white screen. Another man was talking on the platform. The Babbercorns settled at the front, and Old Noshie and Skirty Marm took two rather wobbly chairs near the back.

"Next," said the man on the platform, "possibly the most famous painting in the world – the Mona Lisa, painted by Leonardo da Vinci around the year 1508."

The witches looked with interest at the famous picture, and were a little disappointed that it was only a smiling lady with brown hair. They liked the slide of the Leaning Tower of Pisa much better.

"It began to lean to one side before it was even finished," explained the man on the platform. "Now, this bell tower is one of the wonders of the world."

"It's a BELL TOWER, just like our belfry!" whispered Skirty Marm, impressed.

"I'm glad our belfry doesn't lean over like that," Old Noshie said. "We'd keep sliding out of the windows!"

At the front of the hall, Thomas began to shout, in Babyspeak. "This is BORING! Take me away from this stupid place! I won't stop SHOUTING till you do!"

Mr Babbercorn and Alice did not know Babyspeak, but they understood Thomas's squawks only too well. They put on their raincoats and wheeled the buggy out of the hall. The witches ducked out of sight just in time. Back in the street, the Babbercorns immediately took their raincoats off again. While they had been indoors, watching the slides, the weather had changed. The grey clouds had blown away, leaving the sea and sky bright blue. The whole town gleamed in dazzling sunshine.

"How lovely!" Alice cried. "Let's go down to the beach!"

"Oh, no!" groaned Skirty Marm. "How can we go rainbathing in such DISGUSTING weather?"

Old Noshie did not reply. She had halted beside a large rubbish bin and was staring inside it with eyes and mouth gaping. Someone had thrown away a large brown bottle of NASTY MEDICINE.

Now, as every human knows, drinking someone else's medicine is a very DANGEROUS and STUPID thing to do – almost as bad as taking POISON. To witches, however, Nasty Medicine is a great treat. All it does is make them shockingly tipsy. In the past, Nasty Medicine had got Old Noshie and Skirty Marm into all sorts of trouble, and they had solemnly promised Mr Babbercorn that they would never touch another drop.

"I wish we hadn't made that promise!" Old Noshie sighed now.

"BUM to our promise!" cried Skirty Marm, very rudely. "We're on holiday!"

And (to the amazement of several passers-by) she snatched the bottle of Nasty Medicine out of the bin and took a deep swig.

4

Nutty Golf and a Terrible Donkey

Ten minutes later, Old Noshie and Skirty Marm
were sitting in the gutter outside the Town Hall,
singing loudly:

"Oh, I DO like to be beside the SEASIDE,
Oh, I DO like to be beside the SEA!
Oh, I DO like to peep inside a rubbish BIN
And find some lovely Nasty MED – I –
CINE!"

Old Noshie's brown wig had slipped to one
side, and Skirty Marm had her sunglasses on
upside down. The other people in the street gave
the witches some very funny looks, but they did
not care. I am very sorry to say that they were
disgracefully drunk.

"I've had an idea!" cried Old Noshie. She
only had ideas when she had been at the Nasty
Medicine, and they were never good ideas.
"Let's have a swim!"

The two witches had agreed that they should only swim at night, when there was no danger of anyone seeing them. But that was when they were sober. With a slug of Nasty Medicine inside them, they completely forgot to be sensible.

"*Hahaha*! I'll race yer down to the beach!" yelled Skirty Marm, leaping to her feet.

The holidaymakers and shoppers of Gusty Bay were very alarmed to see what looked like two ancient ladies dashing through the streets, knocking aside anyone who got in their way. Cackling with laughter, the witches ran across the beach to their sleeping place under the pier.

Lots of people had come out to enjoy the beautiful weather, and the beach was crowded. Unknown to the witches, at the other end of the beach Mr Babbercorn and Alice were reading magazines in deck chairs, while Thomas slept in Alice's lap.

"Oh, this is wonderful!" sighed Mr Babbercorn. "I feel as if I haven't a care in the world. I must say, much as I love those witches, things are jolly peaceful without them!"

He would have been horrified if he had guessed what was happening in the damp, shadowy place under the pier. Old Noshie and

Skirty Marm were unpacking their swimming-sacks. They had made themselves these huge things out of the vicar's old shower curtains, which they had found in the shed. The design on the curtains was tropical, with palm trees and pineapples. The witches thought them incredibly smart.

By witch standards, their swimming-sacks were rather revealing. Their heads stuck out at the tops, and you could see nearly all their arms.

"Pretty daring!" giggled Old Noshie tipsily.

"But madly chic!" said Skirty Marm. "If we wore these at Slime Regis, the other witches would go as green as YOU!"

Old Noshie took off her wig, and tied a bin bag over her bald head.

"You'd better cover up your hair," she told Skirty Marm.

"Certainly not," said Skirty Marm, shaking her purple locks. "It's my best feature."

The two witches, in their tropical swimming-sacks, skipped across the sand down to the water's edge. When a wave ran over their toes, they squealed with delight – the sea at Gusty Bay was so much warmer and gentler than the rough sea at Slime Regis. Skirty Marm rushed in at

once and began to swim at top speed – in fact, at about fifty miles an hour, which made every other swimmer near her very frightened.

"Wait for me!" yelled Old Noshie. Sending up a tremendous fountain of spray, she zipped through the water after her friend.

From the shore, it looked as if two speedboats were going berserk. A small crowd began to gather on the sand, and a policeman at the other end of the beach decided to see what was causing the disturbance.

Mr Babbercorn looked up from his magazine. "What's happening over there?"

"Don't worry," Alice said. "It's not your responsibility this time – you're on holiday, and the witches are miles away."

"Hmmm." Mr Babbercorn was thoughtful. "You know, I can't relax – I have the strangest feeling that Old Noshie and Skirty Marm are nearer than we think!"

But before he could investigate, the crowd at the other end of the beach began to break up.

The witches were tired of swimming. Before the policeman could catch up with them, they scurried back to their seaweedy place under the pier and dried themselves by blowing on each other (Old Noshie unfortunately blew on Skirty Marm too hard, and several people nearby had their ice creams puffed right out of the cones). If they had not broken their promise about Nasty Medicine, the witches would have tried to behave, but now all they cared about was having a wild and wicked time.

"Let's try that Nutty Golf!" yelled Old Noshie.

Laughing and biffing each other, they stomped along the promenade to the Crazy Golf course. Old Noshie's make-up had washed off in the sea, and her face glowed like a green traffic light. Skirty Marm had lost her woolly hat, and her hair looked like a clump of purple seaweed. People gasped and stared as these two strange old ladies charged past them – but the witches did not care.

The Crazy Golf course was about the size of a small playground. If you have ever played this game at the seaside, you'll know that people have to knock little balls through model castles and little railways and dragons' tails, with as few hits as possible. That is the whole point of the game. But the witches thought that was boring. To the astonishment of the other people who were playing, Old Noshie and Skirty Marm started whacking their golf balls into each other's mouths. When they were tired of this, Skirty Marm turned all the golf balls into little bombs – whenever anyone hit one, it exploded in a shower of stars. Several people screamed, and one lady fainted.

"OI!" shouted the man in charge. "What do you think you're doing? I'll have the law on you!" He dashed away to fetch the policeman.

Down on the beach, Mr Babbercorn said, "There's a crowd around the Crazy Golf now – maybe I'd better take a look."

Alice only smiled, and gave him a cup of tea from her Thermos flask. "For the last time, stop worrying. We're on holiday!"

The witches had not noticed the chaos they were causing.

"Well, that was a good laugh!" said Skirty Marm, skipping away from the Crazy Golf course before the policeman arrived. "These human holidays are BRILL! What shall we do next?"

"LOOK!" Old Noshie was staring down at the beach, where three grey donkeys were giving children rides on the sand. The witches had never had a donkey-ride, and they were very interested. By a stroke of luck, two donkeys were free. Skirty Marm paid for two rides (even though she was tipsy, she still did not trust Old Noshie with the human money they had borrowed from Mendax). Laughing tremendously, the witches jumped on the backs of their donkeys.

Skirty Marm's donkey was rather young and nervous, and as soon as it felt a witch on its back, it shot across the sand like a firework.

"WHEEE!" shrieked Skirty Marm, as people dived out of the way. "Mine's winning! Hurry up, Noshie!"

Old Noshie was having trouble with her donkey. It was old and fat, with dirty grey hair. If Old Noshie had been looking at its face, she would have seen the animal smiling to itself nastily. It trundled very slowly across the sand.

"Get moving, you smelly old thing!" Old Noshie shouted. "Or I'll turn you into a mouse and EAT you!"

"Oh no you WON'T!" snarled the donkey, to Old Noshie's astonishment.

Just as she was deciding that she must have imagined it, they passed above a small rock

pool, and she saw the donkey's reflection.

A clever witch can disguise herself as anything she likes, but she can't fool any kind of mirror. Her reflection will always show the truth. And the reflection of this donkey made Old Noshie's green face turn deathly pale. When she looked down into the rock pool, she saw the grinning, hideous face of MRS ABERCROMBIE.

Old Noshie was having a ride on the back of the ex-queen of all the witches – the evil old monster who had sworn to kill her!

"Fetch your friend!" growled the donkey. "I want to speak to you both!"

"Shh-tp bibblelibble—" mumbled Old Noshie. She was so frightened, this was all that came out.

When Skirty Marm trotted over, on the back of her real donkey, she found Old Noshie sober as a judge and shaking like a jelly.

"What's the matter with you?" she demanded. "You look as if you've seen a GHOST!"

"She HAS!" said the donkey that was Mrs Abercrombie.

As soon as Skirty Marm saw the reflection in the rock pool, she stopped being cocky. Like Old

Noshie, she turned pale. Unlike Old Noshie, however, she kept her head.

"It's all right, Nosh!" she said. "She hasn't got the Power Hat – she can't hurt us!"

"What does she want?" squeaked Old Noshie.

"Give the donkey-man another fifty pence," said Mrs Abercrombie. "I've got something important to say to you."

The man in charge of the donkeys was rather surprised when Skirty Marm got off her donkey, and said, "We'll have another go with this fat ugly one – but we only want to talk to it."

"Suit yourselves," he said. "It's your money. But watch out, because that one BITES!"

Old Noshie was very glad to get out of the saddle – it was not nice to think of sitting on the back of Mrs Abercrombie.

The donkey led them to a quiet place on the beach, behind a pile of deck chairs. Now that they knew it was the ex-queen in disguise, the witches took a proper look at its face. It had a filthy grey beard, and mean little eyes. When it grinned at them, they saw that its mouth was full of huge METAL TEETH.

"All right," Skirty Marm said, doing her best

to sound very tough and brave. "What's all this about?"

The donkey said, "I want that cat. Get me that cat, or I'll KILL you and your soppy human friends!"

Old Noshie burst into tears.

"The cat-slave Mendax has stolen something that belongs to ME!" said the donkey. Its mouth was foaming with rage, and the cruel expression on its face made both witches shudder. "Ever since you two made my POWER HAT burst into flames, I have been working to win it back!"

"That's impossible," said Skirty Marm. "It's nothing but ashes now!"

"NOW it is," the donkey said, with an unpleasant smile. "But not THEN. You're forgetting your history lessons. Long ago, before the Power Hat was made into the form of a hat, it was a tiny, glowing piece of rock from the Hills Before Time. I have been searching the past for that piece of rock so I can bring it back to the present, and make my Power Hat all over again – just as if you'd never interfered! I traced the Stone back to the BATTLE OF FUNGUS GULCH."

62

Suddenly and very nastily, the donkey that was Mrs Abercrombie scowled. "I nearly had it! It was in my hand! And then a Time Machine landed on my head and squashed me flat – I've still got the tyre-marks on my BUM!"

. The witches gasped. Even Old Noshie understood why the ex-queen was now so angry. By an amazing coincidence, her wicked plan to win back her throne had been foiled by one of Mendax's visits to the Charge of the Pointed Brooms.

"Nobody can resist that Glowing Stone," the donkey said hungrily. "I saw the cat snatch it up, and rush off in a panic!"

"Cor, I'm not surprised!" croaked Old Noshie, her teeth chattering. "Poor old Mendax!"

Skirty Marm was frowning her thinking-frown. "But why have you come after US? If you're so clever, why can't you find Mendax yourself?"

This was obviously a very good question, because Mrs Abercrombie looked furious.

"Because the Glowing Stone has HIDDEN him behind a cloaking-spell!" her donkey-mouth spat out, in a shower of spit. "And my magic isn't strong enough to break it! I'm clever enough to travel through time without one of those stupid, new-fangled Time Machines – but I'm not advanced enough to find my stone."

"The Glowing Stone doesn't want you to find it," Skirty Marm said boldly. "It never liked you when it was a hat! Even far back in time, it thinks you STINK."

"It won't be able to defy me when it's back under my control!" Mrs Abercrombie said. "And you two are going to lead me to it! Tell me where that cat is hiding – before I KILL YOU ALL!"

"Oh, Skirty, what shall we DO?" wailed Old Noshie in terror, thinking of Mr Babbercorn and Alice and little Thomas, only a few metres away.

"Pull yourself together!" ordered Skirty Marm. "As long as Mendax has the sense to hold on to that stone-thing, this nasty old bag can't touch us!"

This made the disguised donkey even more furious. "I'll follow you two to the ends of the earth! I won't rest until I've had my REVENGE! That cat has STOLEN my property!"

"She can't do anything!" cried Skirty Marm.

"Come on, Noshie!"

She grabbed her quaking green friend by the wrist and dashed across the beach towards the pier. The donkey let out a great BREE-HA-HA-HA of rage (if you have ever heard a donkey, you will know how loudly they can scream) and tried to gallop after them. But she could not gallop fast enough.

Old Noshie and Skirty Marm grabbed their broomsticks and witch clothes from under the pier.

"Where are we going?" cried Old Noshie.

Skirty Marm leapt on to her broom. "Quick – we've got to get to Mendax before she does! And I bet I know where he is!"

5

The Chateau Gateau

As soon as the two witches were in the air and Gusty Bay was behind them, Skirty Marm flicked the radio switch on her broom.

"If Mendax was in a panic, he'd have run straight to Mr Snelling – thank goodness he's not at home or Mrs A. would have caught that soppy cat in a second! Tell your broom to fly to the Chateau Gateau, in France!"

Old Noshie was burbling, "Oh deary deary me! Deary me!" over and over again. "Deary dear deary—"

"Calm down at once!" ordered Skirty Marm sternly.

"Oh, Skirty!" cried Old Noshie, "I'm so frightened! She'll catch Mendax and get that stone and make the Power Hat all over again and KILL us and all our friends—"

"CALM DOWN!" yelled Skirty Marm. "We

have to keep our heads. As long as we can find Mendax before she does, we'll have that magic stone. Don't you DARE mess this up!"

It was her strictest voice. Scared as she was, Old Noshie stopped burbling and moaning and made a real effort to be calm. Skirty Marm was very brave, and Old Noshie always followed her in times of danger.

"Sorry, Skirty, I won't," she said humbly.

"We'd better keep radio-silence now," said Skirty Marm, "or Mrs A. will find us too easily."

Both witches turned off their radios. With the wind rushing and roaring in their ears, they flew at top speed across the Channel to France. After about an hour, they saw the rich green fields of Normandy below them. Another twenty minutes, and they were circling above the turrets of a huge, grand castle – the Chateau Gateau, where Mr Snelling was having his posh cooking holiday.

The Chateau was so splendid that Old Noshie almost forgot to be frightened. "Wow, it's like something out of a film! Doesn't the vicar get lost inside it?"

"He's not as SILLY as you are," Skirty Marm said crushingly. "Now, we'd better hide our brooms."

There were some thick bushes near where they had landed. The witches hid their brooms underneath them and scuttled across the velvety lawn to the castle. They crept up to all the windows, peeping inside them one by one. They saw a ballroom, a very grand dining room, and a sitting room full of rather spindly-looking gold chairs.

"I bet they hurt your bottom," said Old Noshie.

"Let's find the kitchens," said Skirty Marm, who was still being very brave and efficient. "Mendax will be wherever the vicar is – and the vicar will be wherever FOOD is!"

The kitchens were at the back of the Chateau Gateau. If the witches had not been so anxious about Mendax and Mrs Abercrombie, they would have stared through the huge windows for hours. There were rows of dazzling stoves, gleaming sinks and shining fridges. There were bowls and whisks and electric mixers, and great simmering pans. It was as big as Mrs Abercrombie's Palace kitchen on Witch Island, but about a million times cleaner, not to mention quieter. Nobody would have dreamt of shouting or biffing here.

A man in a white coat, with a tall white hat, was giving instructions to a class of about twenty-five people. Skirty Marm gave Old Noshie an excited pinch when she saw Mr Snelling among them. He was wearing a striped apron and a tall chef's hat. His round face was anxiously watching the door of a large oven.

The two witches turned themselves into mist, seeped through the open window, and crawled into a big wooden cupboard that ran along the whole length of the room. It was full of very large pots, and they were very cramped when they turned back into solid witches.

Now they could hear the loud voice of the man in white, who was the teacher of the cookery class.

"This is the principle of the perfect soufflé," he was saying bossily. "When you take your soufflés from the oven, they will have puffed up as light as a SIGH – they must rise far above the rim of the dish – tall and spongy, like a chocolate-flavoured CLOUD—"

"I can smell Mendax!" Skirty Marm whispered. Witches have a very sharp sense of smell. "He's here somewhere! Cat – stop hiding! This is an EMERGENCY!"

Out of the dark shadows in the cupboard, they heard a well-known mew.

"Is that you, Skirty?"

Both witches sighed with relief. They were in time – they had reached Mendax before Mrs Abercrombie.

"Of course it's ME," said Skirty Marm. "We knew we'd find you here!"

"You're in a lot of TROUBLE," Old Noshie said, not very helpfully.

From somewhere in the long cupboard, they heard a quavering moan of fear. "I know," Mendax said. "I got the shock of my life when my Time Machine landed on Mrs Abercrombie. Is she after me?"

"She'll probably be here at any moment," whispered Skirty Marm. "We've got to think what to do about that stone-thing – we can't let Mrs A. get it back, so she can make the Power Hat all over again!"

"I lost my head," Mendax admitted. "I was sure she was going to KILL me at once, and I wanted to see my dear vicar once more." His voice was broken by a sob. "He doesn't even know I'm here, but it comforts me to be near him."

Skirty Marm lit the end of her finger (something witches can easily do without hurting themselves) and held it up. The small black head of Mendax was sticking out of one of the enormous pots. He had something lumpy tied up in a dirty handkerchief and fastened to his collar. His green eyes were full of fear.

"Witches, what on earth shall I do?" he mewed. "You've got to help me!"

Even though this was a serious emergency, Skirty Marm could not help feeling rather glad that the snooty talking cat was actually begging her for help. She always enjoyed being in charge.

"Let's get out of here," she hissed. "Follow me!"

Fearfully, Mendax climbed out of his pot. Old Noshie, who was as scared as he was, kindly stroked his back. Skirty Marm peeped out of the cupboard and saw everyone in the class taking their puffy soufflés out of the ovens. She beckoned to the others and crawled out of the cupboard across the stone kitchen floor, towards a handy door. The three of them scuttled out of the door, and Old Noshie slammed it behind her.

In the kitchen, every single soufflé suddenly collapsed.

"Bother and blow! My masterpiece ruined!" grumbled Mr Snelling.

Outside, Mendax took the dirty handkerchief out of his collar and unfolded it.

Old Noshie and Skirty Marm gasped as their eyes were suddenly dazzled by a burst of silver light. The Glowing Stone lay in Mendax's paw, casting its eerie rays around the bushes where they were hiding.

For a long time, they stared at it in silence. There was something sharp and piercing about the light that was partly painful and partly delicious. Their brains felt large and vacant, like empty warehouses waiting to be filled.

"You can't stop looking and looking at it," Mendax whispered. "I just couldn't help picking it up and taking it with me!" He shuddered. "But witches – I can't tell you how scared I was when I found Mrs Abercrombie under my Time Machine!"

"I bet you wish you'd left that funny stone where it was!" said Old Noshie.

Mendax sighed, and shook his head. "If I'd just run away and left the Glowing Stone for Mrs Abercrombie, she would have used it to muck about with history, so that none of us

73

would even have got born! We've got to stop her re-making the Power Hat, or we might as well have ourselves measured for coffins."

There was another long silence while they all stared at the Glowing Stone.

"Well, what are we supposed to DO with the smelly thing?" Old Noshie said crossly. "We can't keep it – we can't hide it—"

"Shhh!" Skirty Marm snapped. She pointed down at the earth, where a very small earwig was making its way between two fallen leaves. "You never know how Mrs A. will disguise herself. This earwig could be her!"

She blew on the palm of her hand, and it turned into a mirror. She held this up above the earwig. Its reflection showed that it was only an earwig.

"Cor, that's a relief!" said Old Noshie, popping it into her mouth.

"You should look on the bright side, Mendax," Skirty Marm said. "You really are a hero now. Never mind Fungus Gulch – this'll get you straight into the Witch Island history books."

Mendax sounded a little more cheerful. "Really? Why?"

"Well, you've saved them from having the old bag back as their queen, haven't you?" said Skirty Marm. "They'll THANK you for nicking that Time Machine now!"

Suddenly, the blue summer sky darkened. A cold wind sprang up, tossing the branches of the trees and stripping the leaves from the bushes where they were hiding. Old Noshie moaned and clutched Skirty Marm's arm.

On the smooth lawn of the Chateau, a speck of black appeared. As they watched, the speck grew and grew – from the size of a conker to the size of a small elephant. Before their terrified eyes, a writhing mass of black smoke slowly took the horrible shape of Mrs Abercrombie.

With shaking paws, Mendax wrapped the Glowing Stone in his handkerchief and tucked it back into his collar.

"We've got to get away!" squeaked Old Noshie.

"Quick, on your broom!" cried Skirty Marm.

"She'd catch your broom in a second and squash you like a fly," Mendax said. "We must run to the old stables where I parked the Time Machine!"

Not fifty metres away, the hideous black

shape of Mrs Abercrombie let out a screech that
shook the earth like thunder.

"GIVE ME MY STONE! YOU'RE ALL
DEAD ANYWAY! YOU'LL NEVER GET
AWAY FROM ME!"

Skirty Marm took a firm hold of Old Noshie's
wrist.

"Now or never!" whispered Mendax.

He dashed across the grass towards the old
stables behind the castle. The witches ran after
him, Old Noshie stumbling and wailing. Mrs
Abercrombie saw them and began to chase
them. It was like being chased by a

thunderstorm. Panting for breath and scared half out of their wits, Mendax and the witches hurtled into the stables and threw themselves at the Time Machine.

"Where? Where?" mewed Mendax, his paws hovering over the controls.

"GIVE ME MY STONE!" Mrs Abercrombie was upon them.

Skirty Marm racked her brains – and remembered the lecture at the Gusty Bay Town Hall. "Italy, 1508!" she yelled. It was the first thing she could think of, though she had not a clue what it meant. Neither witch knew much about human history.

Mendax pulled the switch, and they were off.

A ride in a Time Machine is an extraordinary thing. You feel as if you are falling, falling, falling, with the centuries rushing through your hair, and all the noises of the years babbling around you.

They landed, with a tremendous jolt, in brilliant sunshine.

"Phew!" said Skirty Marm. "She'll never find us here!"

Meanwhile, back in Gusty Bay, Mr Babbercorn

and Alice were enjoying beautiful weather. They had spent a whole, lazy day on the beach, and were making their way back to the Sea Breeze Guest House, feeling very happy and sandy and pleasantly tired.

"I'm sorry I was fussing this morning," Mr Babbercorn said to Alice. "I couldn't stop worrying about the witches, but now I feel I've really got away from it all."

"The newspaper says the weather's going to be gorgeous," Alice said cheerfully. "Thomas will be as brown as a little nut when we get home!"

Mr Babbercorn chuckled. "And we won't have to sit through another of those lectures in the Town Hall!"

He would have been very surprised if he could have seen the changes that had come over the lecturer's box of slides. Next time it rained, the audience would hear about the peculiar things that had happened in Northern Italy, back in 1508. They would see pictures of the *Upright* Tower of Pisa, and the world's most famous painting – the MONA NOSHIE.

6

The Mona Noshie

The witches and Mendax lay in the hot sun, weak with relief that – so far – Mrs Abercrombie had not followed them. Mendax was the first to recover. He jumped out of the Time Machine. His voice had almost returned to its usual coolness.

"Listen, witches – I'm very sorry I got into such a panic. It was really very decent of you to come to the Chateau Gateau and take me away. I would have hated anything bad to happen to dear Mr Snelling." He smoothed his whiskers and patted the bulging handkerchief tucked into his collar. "Now, we must find somewhere safe to hide this stone."

Skirty Marm was trying to work out all kinds of complicated things to do with Time. "Shouldn't you put it back where it was, at Fungus Gulch?" she asked.

Mendax shook his head. "I've already thought of that. Mrs Abercrombie will go back and snatch it. She can only muck about with history if she has the Stone, so we have to hide it where she can't possibly find it. Then we'll get born, and the Power Hat will get burned, and things will be just the same."

"Easier said than done," Skirty Marm said. "What do you think, Noshie?"

"Eh?" Old Noshie had not heard a word of this. She was staring around with eyes like saucers.

They were in a grove of little olive trees, gnarled and twisted like gnomes. Beautiful fields stretched around it, shimmering in the heat. Below them, in the distance, they saw a magnificent city, full of sparkling white buildings.

"How exquisite!" purred elegant Mendax. "Florence in the early sixteenth century – at the very height of the Italian Renaissance!"

"What are you talking about?" Old Noshie asked crossly. "Speak Hinglish!"

Mendax sniffed haughtily. "I wouldn't expect an uncultured witch like you to appreciate this experience, but let me tell you, many a human would give their eye-teeth to be here!"

"Well, I'd give my eye-teeth and my EAR-teeth to get away from here," said Old Noshie. "I don't see what's so great about being chased by an evil fat monster!"

Skirty Marm had a little more feeling for culture than her green friend. "Maybe we'll find somewhere good to hide the Glowing Stone," she said. "Mendax, is there any way we can take a look around? We left our brooms in France."

"Pooh!" swore Old Noshie, who had forgotten this.

"There's a travel-button on the Time Machine," Mendax said, jumping back into the driver's seat. "Let's take a little tour and soak up the atmosphere." He pressed a button neatly with his paw. The dashboard opened and a steering-wheel popped up. The Time Machine soared into the warm sky, and the witches leaned rather dangerously out of their seats to gape at the wonderful view.

"Look!" shouted Old Noshie, "There's that broken bell tower we saw in the Town Hall!"

The Time Machine was circling gracefully above the famous Leaning Tower of Pisa. Because they lived in a bell tower themselves, the witches were very interested in this tall white tower, leaning to one side.

"It looks a bit windy," Skirty Marm said. "We'd need two pairs of bloomers in the winter if we had to live up there!"

"I think it's great!" cried Old Noshie. "Can't we stop and have a proper look? Oh, PLEASE!"

"If we stay in the air too long, it'll be easier for Mrs A. to spot us!" Skirty Marm pointed out. She was just as keen to examine the strange tower, which looked very much like the

ramshackle buildings of Witch Island.

Mendax landed the Time Machine on the wide open space in front of the Leaning Tower. This was hundreds of years before the invention of the aeroplane, and the people of Pisa were very frightened to see the Time Machine appearing out of the air above them. They were even more frightened when they saw its passengers. A noisy crowd gathered to stare at them – but from a long way off.

"*Heeheehee*! Look at their BONKERS CLOTHES!" yelled Skirty Marm.

They had never seen pictures of the clothes worn by humans in olden times and thought these were hilarious.

"The men are wearing STOCKINGS!" laughed Old Noshie. "And their hats look like CABBAGES! Hahahaha!"

"Oh, do pull yourselves together," Mendax muttered crossly. "Have you no feeling for history?"

Old Noshie climbed out of the Time Machine and looked up at the Leaning Tower.

"I don't like it, Skirt. It makes me ever so giddy."

A brilliant idea came to Skirty Marm. "I

know – let's STRAIGHTEN it! Won't they be pleased?"

"Are you crazy?" Mendax gasped indignantly.

But Skirty Marm was already standing beside Old Noshie. Witches are incredibly strong and all they had to do was push hard, with both hands. Before long, the Leaning Tower of Pisa was standing up straight. The people of Pisa screamed with terror. Also with anger, because the Tower was already a popular tourist attraction – and who would come to visit the Upright Tower of Pisa?

"You'll thank us for this later!" Skirty Marm shouted at them. She got back into the Time Machine. "Come on, Noshie. Humans are so ungrateful sometimes."

"You've destroyed one of the wonders of the world," spat Mendax. "I hope you're SATISFIED!"

Before the angry citizens of Pisa could rush at them, the Time Machine took off again. The tower – now standing as upright as an exclamation mark – fell away behind them.

"I'm hungry," Old Noshie complained. "I keep thinking about that puffy chocolate thing the vicar was making!"

Mendax sighed. "I have some sandwiches in the glove compartment. I suppose we had better stop for a rest."

They were above the city of Florence now. Mendax landed the Time Machine in farmland on the outskirts and hid it carefully in a haystack, not wanting to attract any more attention. Unfortunately, they looked extremely odd to the humans they met. The witches were still wearing their human old-lady disguises from Gusty Bay. And green skin and purple hair look odd practically everywhere.

In the narrow, crowded streets of the city, they were careful to stick to the darkest places. Eventually, when their stomachs were rumbling terribly, they found a deserted alley. Skirty Marm took Mendax's sandwiches out of her coat pocket and divided them into three rather small portions.

"Huh! Fish-paste again!" she grumbled, with her mouth full.

Suddenly, a door opened in the alley. Out came an old man, with a long white beard. At first, he was shocked to see what were obviously two witches – as all humans are. But slowly, he seemed to become fascinated with the green face of Old Noshie. He stared at her with very bright, sharp eyes, until Old Noshie began to get annoyed.

"He's after my sandwiches! Go away, you nasty man! Shoo!"

The old man gabbled something at them in a strange language.

"Good gracious!" mewed Mendax, astonished. "It must be because I'm wearing the Glowing Stone – I can understand him!" He listened for a moment. "He says he's a painter. The lady he was going to paint is late – and anyway, he doesn't want her any more. He wants to paint Old Noshie instead."

"What colour?" asked Skirty Marm.

"I like being green!" shouted Old Noshie.

Mendax rolled his eyes impatiently. "Noshie, must you be such a PEASANT? He wants to paint a picture of you!"

"Of ME?" Nobody had ever wanted a picture of Old Noshie before, and she was flattered – particularly when she saw Skirty Marm's jealous scowl. "All right!"

"He could be Mrs A. in disguise!" Skirty Marm muttered. "We'll all be killed, just because you're a SHOW-OFF!"

"Bum to you!" smirked Old Noshie.

Mendax was also jealous – he was very vain. "I can't think why he wants a painting of a HAIRLESS SPROUT," he sniffed, "but he says he'll give us some food, so let's go inside."

The old man seemed excited. He led them into his house, and said something to a lady. (Skirty Marm remembered to check the lady's reflection in her mirror-hand.) The lady began to spread a table with cakes and pies and delicious bread. Then it was Old Noshie's turn to be annoyed – she could not eat anything because the old man made her sit still to have her portrait painted. Old Noshie was a fidgety witch, and she was hungry. She looked at the food so longingly that Skirty Marm forgave her for being painted and stored a couple of pies in her pocket to eat later.

At last, the painting (that should have been the Mona Lisa, and was now the Mona Noshie) was finished. The lady came back and said something to the old man.

Mendax translated. "She says there's a cardinal come to sit for his portrait." He stiffened suddenly. "But the old man says he's not expecting anyone. I don't like the sound of that!"

Taking care to stay hidden, Skirty Marm ran to the top of the stairs. At the bottom stood a stout man in a bright red dress. He looked very important, and his hands were covered with glittering rings. But Skirty Marm saw his reflection in her mirror-hand – and nearly screamed aloud. She rushed to her friends.

"It's HER! We've got to get out!"

"What about my PIE?" moaned Old Noshie. The other two ignored her. Skirty Marm grabbed Noshie's hand, and Mendax pulled at her coat with his teeth. Together they jumped out of the window, just as the heavy footsteps of

Mrs Abercrombie were heard on the stairs. They ran out of the alley and quickly hid inside an old barrel.

It had been a very close shave. They stayed in the barrel until it got dark, to have a better chance of escaping without Mrs Abercrombie seeing them. Mendax discovered that he could instruct the Glowing Stone to hide them from the humans, but Mrs Abercrombie was horribly clever, and Mendax wasn't absolutely sure the Stone could conceal them from her.

At the dead of night, very scared and very tired, they finally returned to the haystack where they had parked the Time Machine.

"I want to go HOME!" wailed Old Noshie.

"Stop that grizzling!" spat Mendax crossly. "We can't!"

"Hang on!" cried Skirty Marm. "I've had an idea! Jump in, both of you!" She leapt into the driver's seat.

"I can't imagine what you're doing, and I don't care," Mendax said, fastening his seat belt. "If either of you survive me, I'd like a very quiet funeral. The dear vicar might like to have me stuffed."

Skirty Marm – very excited – was turning the

dials on the dashboard. Then she pulled the switch, and they were thrown back into the rushing stream of Time.

After a while, they halted. To the amazement and horror of Mendax, they were back in the garden shed at the vicarage.

"You IDIOT!" he groaned. "She'll find us in about thirty seconds! We're all going to DIE! And by the way, you owe me money – OW!"

Skirty Marm had pushed the small cat roughly out of the Time Machine. She shoved Old Noshie out after him, and jumped out herself. Suddenly, there was a tremendous clap of thunder that made the whole shed shake as if it were made of tissue paper.

Mrs Abercrombie had crashed down in the vicarage garden.

Old Noshie bellowed with fear and hid her face in her hat. Skirty Marm, however, stayed calm. She plucked the handkerchief out of Mendax's collar and shut it in the glove compartment of the Time Machine. Then she did something very brave – possibly the bravest thing she had ever done in the whole of her brave career. She turned the dials on the dashboard to their highest settings, pulled the switch and jumped out of the Time Machine a split second before it vanished into thin air.

In the stunned silence that followed, Mendax sat up, rubbing his shoulder. Old Noshie finally dared to take her face out of her hat. There was nothing but dusty empty space where the Time Machine had been.

Skirty Marm was very pale. Sparks flew from the ends of her purple hair, and it stood out like a brush. "I've sent the Glowing Stone heaven-knows-WHERE, and heaven-knows-WHEN!" she said breathlessly. "It will whirl round in SPACE for ever – she'll have to go through the whole UNIVERSE with a comb to find it now!"

"That was exceedingly bright of you, Skirty Marm," said Mendax. "And under the circum-stances, you can keep the money."

Old Noshie began to tremble. A black, conker-sized speck was hovering in the corner of the shed, above the lawnmower. Once again, as they watched, it swelled and writhed and took the disgusting form of Mrs Abercrombie.

The lightning flashed and the thunder rolled, until the skies above Tranters End seemed about to split open. The ex-queen of the witches already knew what had happened to the

Glowing Stone. She was so furious that her skin was smoking all over.

"I WILL HAVE MY HAT!" she roared. "AND WHEN I GET IT BACK, I WILL HAVE MY REVENGE! AAAARGH!"

There was a deafening crash. The witches and Mendax were lifted off their feet and landed in a hot shower of dust and soil. When they had stopped coughing and spluttering, they gazed around them in astonishment.

A sweet and peaceful silence had fallen upon the village of Tranters End. But there was no garden shed at the vicarage any more – no rowing machine, no lawnmower, no deck chairs, no old tins of paint. Old Noshie, Skirty Marm and Mendax were sitting on the bald, blackened piece of earth where it had been.

"Blimey!" murmured Skirty Marm, very impressed. "She was so angry, she EXPLODED!"

Mendax staggered up on shaking paws. "I think I'll put the kettle on."

Old Noshie sniffed. "I wish Mr B. and Alice were here. I don't even care if they're cross about the shed. I just want to see them, to make sure they're safe!"

And at that moment, Mr Babbercorn's voice called from the house, "Witches! Mendax! Good grief – where's the shed?"

There, at the back door, was Mr Babbercorn, with Alice behind him and Thomas in her arms. They all looked very brown and healthy. The weedy curate had grown a little fatter.

"But what are they doing here?" wondered Skirty Marm. "They're not due back for another two weeks!"

"You must have set the Time Machine to the wrong day when we came back," Mendax said. "And I'm glad you did – if the Babbercorns are home now, that means my dear Mr Snelling will be back this afternoon!"

The three of them waved to Mr Babbercorn and Alice and began to hurry towards the house.

"You know," Old Noshie said, "I think being without us has done them a lot of good. Look how pleased they are to see us again!"

"They've missed us!" Skirty Marm said proudly. "Maybe we were wrong to follow them on their holiday. Maybe we should let them go away by themselves again next year." She sighed. "I'm sorry we had to leave those rubber rings at Gusty Bay!"

"I'll let you wear my spade sometimes," offered Old Noshie, who still had this beautiful object tied round her neck. "After all, you were very brave."

Mr Babbercorn had had such a delightful holiday that he was only a little irritated about the shed. Mr Snelling – who had had a marvellous time at the Chateau Gateau – did not mind either.

"I'm glad that rowing machine's gone," he declared. "It made me feel guilty every time I went in there."

The witches decided not to tell Mr Babbercorn about Gusty Bay and the Nasty Medicine – but they did tell the whole story to Chancellor Badsleeves, their old friend, who was now the leader of Witch Island. As Skirty Marm had predicted, she forgave Mendax for stealing the Time Machine. The explosion of Mrs Abercrombie had caused great rejoicing amongst the witches, and the Chancellor solemnly declared a National Explosion Day every year, to be celebrated with fireworks. She also promised to send a crack Time-squad to clear up the bits of human history the witches had damaged.

Old Noshie did not mind too much about her portrait disappearing from history.

"But they needn't have changed everything back!" she declared. "I still think that tower looks better when it's STRAIGHT!"

Kate Saunders
BELFRY WITCHES 1
A Spell of Witches

Old Noshie and Skirty Marm have committed a terrible crime. They've sung a frightfully rude song about Mrs Abercrombie, Queen of the Witches, at the Hallowe'en Ball. Now they are to be banished from Witch Island for ever!

Where can two wacky witches find a new home? The sleepy village of Tranters End is about to get a bewitching surprise . . .

Kate Saunders
BELFRY WITCHES 2
Mendax the Mystery Cat

Old Noshie and Skirty Marm have been trying terribly hard to be good.
They've only done the tiniest bit of magic, they haven't touched a drop
of Nasty Medicine, and they've even been learning how to knit!

But strange powers are at work in Tranters End. First there's the
underwear that comes to life, then the flying pigs – and then a very
mysterious black cat arrives at the vicarage door . . .

Kate Saunders
BELFRY WITCHES 3
Red Stocking Rescue

Old Noshie and Skirty Marm are terribly upset. Although they've
promised to be good, Mr Babbercorn won't let them be
bridesmaids at his wedding. And Mendax the cat isn't even
allowed to sing a solo!

But then deep, dark magic turns Alice, Mr Babbercorn's bride-to-
be, into a snail. Who is the culprit – and can two brave witches
(and one clever cat) cook up a spell that will save the wedding
from disaster?

Kate Saunders
BELFRY WITCHES 6
Broomsticks in Space

A strange light has been seen in the night sky over Tranters End. Could
it be a new planet? Maybe that would explain the weird weather – surely
snow in summer isn't normal!

Something very dirty and dangerous is afoot, and Old Noshie and
Skirty Marm are certain who's to blame – none other than their old
enemy Mrs Abercrombie. For the deadliest witch of all has moved
her operations to outer space, and this time she's cooking up a king-
sized cauldron of trouble!

Collect all the BELFRY WITCHES books!

The prices shown below are correct at the time of going to press.
However, Macmillan Publishers reserve the right to show new retail
prices on covers which may differ from those previously advertised.

All Macmillan titles can be ordered at your local bookshop
or are available by post from:

**Book Service by Post
PO Box 29, Douglas, Isle of Man IM99 1BQ**

Credit cards accepted. For details:
Telephone: 01624 675137
Fax: 01624 670923
E-mail: bookshop@enterprise.net

Free postage and packing in the UK.
Overseas customers: add £1 per book (paperback)
and £3 per book (hardback).